INSPIRING STORIES
FOR AMAZING GIRLS

Eva Kinsley

Content

Introduction

Hey! It's wonderful that you have taken the time to read this book. I'm sure you're already curious about what's in store for you. But first, I want to tell you a secret. It's a very important secret that can accompany you throughout your life. So, pay close attention and read the following lines carefully.

Do you know that you are very special? Although there are millions of boys and girls

in this world, there is only one of you.
No one is exactly like you. You are
completely unique, and you should always
remember that. When life becomes difficult,
you must always remember you are unique
and important to this world just the way you
are.

Sometimes, life is not easy; there are many
small and big challenges in our lives.
Every obstacle requires self-awareness,
courage, and self-confidence.
Sometimes, you may think you can't solve a
problem. Maybe you will even feel terrified
and doubt yourself. The truth is: everyone
feels this way from time to time. Even adults!

Yes, you heard right. Mom, Dad, Grandma,
Grandpa, and even your teachers sometimes
miss courage and confidence. So, become

brave, don't give up, and never lose faith in yourself.

Every day is full of surprises. There are many wonderful days you probably wish would never end. Sooner or later, every person will experience days when not everything goes according to plan. Things will happen that make us very sad, scared, or even angry. These bad days are also a part of life. There can be no joy in life without bad experiences. Without the bad, we can't fully appreciate the good.

This book has many stories where you will meet wonderful girls. Girls who overcome their fears. Girls who are brave. Girls who show inner strength. You can do all of this too. You must believe in yourself. I hope these stories help you do so.

In the following pages, small and big dreams come true.

PS: After each story, you will find a mandala with a special message. You can color the mandala, especially with many different bright colors. Take your time and enjoy the process. Coloring the mandala will help you remember the message better.

Have fun reading!

I am special!

Mia and the Squirrel

The alarm clock rang and pulled Mia out of a deep dream. She yawned loudly. Sleepily, she rubbed her eyes. Mia was a cheerful girl with long brown hair. She turned eight last week. She was in the second grade.

Mia stretched and wiggled a bit in bed, and then slowly stood up. She went to the window of her room and carefully pushed aside the yellow curtains. Then, she opened the window. It was seven in the morning, and the first rays of the sun lit up the room. The fresh morning air flowed toward her.

She took a deep breath and looked out the window at the big trees and the many flowers that bloomed on the lawn. It was a beautiful morning, but Mia still didn't feel well that day. She loved warm summer days. Usually, she couldn't wait to run outside to soak up the sunshine in the backyard. But, today, she preferred to stay inside.

Mia wandered restlessly around her room for a while. Finally, she made up her mind, put on her favorite blue dress, and made her bed. She also packed her bag with notebooks and books to prepare her for school.

Mia also didn't forget to take her gym bag. Crammed inside the bag were track pants, a T-shirt, and tennis shoes. On Fridays, she had gym class during the last hour.

Usually, Mia loved this hour, but today everything was completely different.

Last week, Mia's teacher, Mrs. Peterson, announced they would use the climbing rope in the next gym class. Mia felt terrified. She had never climbed anywhere in her life. With a lump in her throat, she thought about her classmates. If she failed, then they would laugh at her, or even call her mean names. Hundreds of thoughts raced through Mia's head, and she felt dizzy.

Suddenly, there was a knock at her door. It was Mia's mom. She wanted to know if she was awake. "I'm coming, Mom!" shouted Mia. Her mom opened the door and said, "Good morning, my darling. Breakfast is ready! It's getting late and school will start soon!".

"Just a minute!" replied Mia. She swung her bag onto her back and reached for her gym bag with her right hand.

As she was about to close the window in her room, Mia heard a loud rustling sound outside. Curious, she looked where the noise was coming from. That's when she saw it! A small, reddish-brown squirrel was nimbly climbing a large tree in the backyard. Hurriedly, it reached the top of the tree.

"Oh, if only I could climb as well as you

do, little squirrel. Then, the climbing rope would be easy for me, and I wouldn't have to be afraid anymore ..." Mia sighed softly to herself.

With a frown, she closed the window and made her way to the kitchen.

Mom had already prepared breakfast there. There were fresh rolls with delicious strawberry jam and hot chocolate to drink. Dad was already sitting at the table, happily drinking his coffee while he read the newspaper.

Mia was not hungry, because she felt

anxious. However, Mom always said it was important not to leave the house without eating breakfast. So, with a heavy heart, Mia ate a small roll covered with jam. After all, she didn't want to feel hungry during class. "So, what's on the agenda for school today?" asked Dad.

Mia quickly swallowed her last bite and answered, "First I have math, then English, and finally gym class!"

For a moment, Mia thought she might tell her parents about her fear of the climbing rope. She decided against it.

Somehow, she didn't want to talk to Mom and Dad about it, now. Although, she usually talked everything over with them.
After breakfast, she ran to the bathroom,

carefully brushed her teeth, and combed her long hair with the brush. Then she said goodbye to her parents, who gave her a kiss on the forehead and wished her a good day at school.

Mia made her way to the bus. The bus stop was only a few minutes from Mia's house. She heard a rustling sound again. Then, she saw the squirrel from before. It had a nut in its hands and was only a few feet away from Mia. The squirrel also noticed the girl. It stood on its hind legs and gazed deeply into Mia's eyes. "You're not going to take my nut, are you?" the squirrel asked cheekily.

Mia stood in front of the cute animal with her jaw on the floor and her eyes wide. She was unable to believe what was happening. Did the squirrel really speak to her or was she dreaming?

"You ... you ... you can talk?" stuttered Mia in disbelief.

"Yes, I can, but I rarely actually talk to people. For you, today, I'll make an exception, dear Mia, because I like you!" replied the squirrel.

"Hh...Hh...how do you know my name?" asked Mia in complete amazement.

"Well, we are neighbors! I've been living on that birch tree over there for some time. From there, I sometimes watch you play with your friends or talk to your parents. That's how I learned your name.

Where are my manners? My name is Frederik, but you can call me Fred. Tell me, you kids have to go to school in the morning, right? I think you need to leave soon!" said the squirrel.

"Hello, Fred. It's nice to meet you!" Mia replied with a smile. Then, she continued with a slightly hushed and more serious tone, "Well, actually, I don't want to go to school today. I'm supposed to climb the climbing rope in gym class, and I'm terrified of it." "But, Mia, you don't have to be scared of that at all. Take a deep breath and don't look down. You'll figure out that it's not that hard!" said Fred, smiling and nodding his tiny head to try to cheer Mia up.

"Well, that's easy for you to say. After all, you're a squirrel and you're naturally great at climbing. But, Fred, I can't!" sighed Mia in frustration. Fred felt sorry for the little girl. He scratched his head with his right hand and pondered about how he could help Mia.

Then he started to say: "Yes, you are absolutely right. Today, I can climb really well, but, you know, I wasn't like that from the start. I remember when I was a little baby squirrel. The first time I had to climb a tree by myself, I was as scared as you are now. Honestly, it's okay to feel scared and nervous about new things, but you shouldn't let it stop you.

If you really want to climb that rope, then you have to believe in yourself.
I, for one, believe in you. You can do it!"

Mia listened intently to Fred. While listening, she discovered a new, overwhelming sense of courage. Fred was right. She could do it if she believed in herself. She would have liked to chat with him some more, but now she really had to hurry to school.

"Thank you for your help, Fred. I will remember what you said. You helped me a lot. I hope to see you again soon."
Hastily, she waved to Fred. He had already dashed back up the tree trunk. He glanced briefly at Mia, and then he disappeared into the dense branches. With a renewed courage to face life, Mia got on the bus and went to school. She decided to face her fear.

"Brrrring!" rang the school bell. The time had finally come for Mia to climb the dreaded climbing rope. Mia could hardly concentrate on her classwork that morning. She couldn't stop thinking about Fred and his words.

It was 11 o'clock, and it was time for her gym class to begin. The children walked with their teacher, Mrs. Peterson, to the gymnasium, which was right next to the school building. After everyone had changed into their gym clothes, they gathered in front of the climbing rope. Mrs. Peterson said to the children, "As we discussed last week, we are going to climb up the climbing rope."

Before they started climbing, everyone had to do warm up exercises. Then, they lined up. One by one, they climbed the rope. Some climbed quickly and skillfully, but others climbed slowly and carefully. Mia's heart began to beat faster and faster. She gazed reluctantly at the long rope she needed to master. To prevent injuries, soft blue mats laid on the floor in front of them. This calmed Mia down a bit, but she still felt nervous. The rope was not particularly high, but to Mia, it seemed like mount Everest. She stood at the very back of the line, so she could watch the other children conquer the rope first. Mia realized many of the other children also seemed anxious.

Then, it was her turn. Immediately, her heart began to pound out of her chest, but she couldn't give up now. Not under any circumstances. She had to, at least, try to do her best. She thought again about Fred's words and finally walked toward the rope. Mia closed her eyes for a moment and took another deep breath. Then, she began to climb. The first part was difficult, and her feet trembled a little bit. Nevertheless, with each pull and push, it felt easier and easier. Mia continued to climb. With excitement, she wondered how high she had climbed. She was curious and tried to catch a glimpse, but, then, she remembered Fred's advice: don't look down!

She paused briefly and gathered her strength again. She went a bit farther and finally reached the top. After a short pause, she carefully climbed down until she felt her feet touch the ground again. She made it!

A feeling of joy and pride rose within her.
A big grin lit up her face as she beamed with pride and happiness.

"That was great how you climbed to the top, Mia. Almost as graceful as a squirrel!"
Mrs. Peterson praised the girl and winked at her as if she knew about her mentor the squirrel.

After gym class, Mia headed home with Eva. She would have loved to tell Eva the story of her new furry friend, but Mia kept her special little secret. Still, Mia seemed to be in a daydream.
She skipped the rest of the way home, thinking over and over about how she mastered the climbing rope. She felt free and overjoyed. Once she arrived home, Mia couldn't wait to tell Fred. He had to be the

first to know. So, she ran into the backyard and stopped right under the birch tree.

"Fred, where are you?" the girl called, looking around in all directions. Again and again, she called out as loud as she could, and she didn't care if anyone heard her. She had to tell him.

Suddenly, Fred came running. His bushy tail wagged back and forth. He stood in front of her, looking at her questioningly.
"Fred, there you are at last! You won't believe it! I climbed all the way to the top. I could never have done it without your advice. Thanks for your help!" Mia said beaming with joy. She wanted to take the cute little animal in her arms. Fred reared back a little and replied, "You're welcome, but you have only yourself to thank for that.

After all, you were the one climbing that rope, not me. I was just giving you advice. I was convinced you would make it. I am also quite sure that you will achieve so much more in your life.

You must simply believe in yourself. Now, I must continue collecting nuts and seeds for the winter. Goodbye and see you soon."

Mia wanted to talk more with Fred. But, before she knew it, Fred gracefully climbed another tree and disappeared behind the branches and leaves.

It took Mia a moment to understand her new friend's words. She still felt as if she were caught in a beautiful dream.
Fred was right. She climbed alone, and she had done it because she conquered her fear. Still, Fred was a great help to her, and, for that, she felt grateful. With a smile, Mia looked up at the tree once more, hoping to catch a glimpse of Fred. However, Fred had already jumped to another tree and was busy looking for supplies for the winter.

Today, Mia learned she could do more by herself than she initially thought. So much was possible if she only believed in herself.

Who knows? Maybe Mia would become a mountaineer and climb Mount Everest?

Whatever her life might be in the future, she would never forget this day.

Thank you, Fred!

30

I am proud of myself !

The Test of Courage

Do you know what a dare is? Maybe you've heard about it at some point. In a so-called test of courage, you are supposed to do something and overcome your fear.

For example, letting a spider crawl on your hand, touching a stinging nettle, or even eating an earthworm. Yuck! This story is about a similar test of courage.

Victoria was ten years old and in the fourth grade. She was an extremely cheerful girl. At school, she had two very good friends. Their names were Charlotte and Hannah, and they were in the same class as Victoria. The three girls liked to meet after school, and they spent a lot of time together. They did their homework together, played card games, and goofed around. Today, once again, they met at Victoria's home.

After playing Uno in the apartment for an hour, they decided to go outside. It was a mid-August afternoon, and it was pleasantly warm. Only a few small clouds covered the bright sun. Birds chirped merrily from the trees.

Victoria lived with her parents outside the city in a rural area with many trees, bushes, and meadows full of flowers. Occasionally, sheep and cows grazed in the meadows.

For a few weeks, the three girls challenged each other with dares when alone in nature. Charlotte and Hannah came up with wild ideas. Victoria, by contrast, was not fond of most of the dares. However, she didn't dare to tell her friends. After all, she didn't want to be called a chicken or look like a negative Nancy. That's why Victoria had participated in every dare.

As the girls walked past a tall walnut tree, Charlotte once again had an idea for a new dare.

Full of enthusiasm, Charlotte said to Victoria and Hannah: "I just thought of a dare.
See that big tree over there? Which one of you dares to climb up there?"

Victoria gulped. She frowned thoughtfully.

Climbing such a tall tree was not something she was comfortable with. She gathered all her courage and decided to speak her mind, "Well, I don't think that's a good idea. If you fell from that height, then you could break every bone in your body! There's no way I'm going to climb up there, and I hope you guys don't either! Climbing a tree that tall is way too risky!"

For the very first time, Victoria spoke up about how she really felt.

"Are you scared?" asked Charlotte with a mischievous grin.

"You sound like a scaredy-cat! Victoria is a scaredy-cat!" exclaimed Hannah in a loud voice.

For Victoria, it hurt that Charlotte and Hannah were making fun of her. She still stuck to her decision to not climb the tree. It was simply way too dangerous.

Charlotte now went to the tree and said confidently, "All right. Then, I'll show the scaredy-cat that it's not so bad to climb this tree. Now, pay attention and take notes!"

Then, Charlotte began to climb. Branch by branch, she pulled herself higher and higher. With every step she took, the branches cracked, and they grew thinner the further up she climbed. Broken branches fell to the ground. When Charlotte reached the halfway point, she climbed onto a thicker branch to take a short break. From there, she looked down at Victoria and Hannah.
"Look at how high I am! I told you there's nothing to be afraid of. This is totally easy!" cheered Charlotte.

But then it suddenly happened!
Out of sheer joy, Charlotte relaxed for a
moment, and she lost her balance. With all
her might, she tried to hold on to a branch,
but it was too late. She fell from the tree and
landed on the ground with a big thump.

"Ouch!" moaned
Charlotte in pain.
She had fallen
directly on her right
thigh. Immediately,
Victoria and Hannah
ran to help her.
"Are you all right?
Are you in pain?"
asked Victoria
worriedly. "I think I broke my leg. Also, I
feel so dizzy. I need a doctor. Help me,
please!" sobbed Charlotte with tears running

down her face. Victoria didn't hesitate for a moment and ran home as fast as she could.

She frantically told her mother about what happened to Charlotte. Victoria's mother dialed 911 and called for help. Then, Victoria ran back to the scene of the accident as quickly as her little legs could carry her. She wanted to wait for the ambulance with Charlotte and Hannah.

About ten minutes later, the paramedics arrived. He was wearing a yellow and red paramedic suit and carried an emergency medical pack with him so he could examine Charlotte closely. He carefully palpated her leg and then said, "I think it would be best to X-ray your leg at the hospital."
Using a blue, ice-cold plastic bag, he cooled the injured leg to reduce the swelling.

Charlotte was carefully carried into the ambulance and driven to the hospital. Hannah and Victoria accompanied her to offer their support.

While the three girls waited for the X-ray, Charlotte said to Victoria, "You were right. This was a stupid dare. I should have listened to you, but, instead, I laughed at you. I'm so sorry! Thank you for calling an ambulance for me so quickly.

You are a really great friend!"
Hannah also apologized to Victoria, "I'm also sorry for calling you a scaredy-cat earlier. That was mean of me, and it was not okay."

"It's okay. We all make mistakes sometimes. Besides, we're best friends after all! Apology accepted!" replied Victoria with a reassuring smile on her face.

Now, the doctor came back. He held a large X-ray in his hand, showing Charlotte's thigh.

"You're lucky, Charlotte. You bruised your leg badly, but it's not broken! You have to rest your leg for a while and apply a special ointment. In two to three weeks, your leg should be fully recovered. Just don't do any more dangerous things," the doctor warned.

Immediately, the three girls breathed a sigh of relief. Thank God nothing worse had happened to Charlotte.

Victoria was glad she listened to her heart. Courage means daring to do something, but safety and assessing whether something might be too dangerous is also important. You don't always have to play the superhero to show courage. It also shows courage to say "no" when you don't want to do something.

Sometimes, you show more courage by saying "no" than by being brave and doing something dangerous. Victoria showed true courage and bravery by speaking her mind and standing up for what she believed in.

I trust myself!

A Bad Day

Anna sat nervously in her seat. She glanced at the door. Soon, Mr. Smith would come into the classroom and begin the English lesson. Hectically, she drew a sunflower in her sketchbook. Anna always drew when she felt anxious. The process helped distract her. Today, that didn't work out. Her stress was too great.

Anna sat next to her friend Lydia. The two met in kindergarten and became good friends. Now, they went to the same class and were seat neighbors.

Anna said to Lydia, "Today, we'll get our grades from last week's test. I don't have a good feeling. I made a lot of mistakes, and the test was pretty hard."

Unlike Anna, Lydia didn't seem anxious. Lydia always made straight A's in English and probably expected a very good grade in this test. Lydia looked at Anna with a surprised expression and said, "Well, I thought the test was pretty easy!"

That was exactly what Anna didn't want to hear right now. Nonetheless, she would be happy for her friend if she got an A again. Secretly, Anna wished Lydia had agreed the test wasn't easy.

With long strides, Mr. Smith entered the classroom. He placed his large brown briefcase on the desk. Then, he greeted the students in a cheery mood, "What a wonderful morning! I have finally corrected last week's test. I'm sure you're all anxious to see what grades you've received."

A loud murmur passed through the classroom among the students.
Apparently, Anna was not the only one who would prefer to never find out what she scored on her test.
Some students whispered frantically. Others stared silently at the floor, playing with their pencil cases or biting their fingernails.

Mr. Smith took a stack of papers out of his folder. As under a spell, the students paid close attention to every word Mr. Smith said, "There is only one A, four B's, eight C's. Two D's and also, unfortunately, an F!"

Anna's stomach dropped. She felt sick at the thought that she might have the F. Her face turned ghostly white. She definitely didn't want to have the only F, but she now feared the worst.

Mr. Smith began to go through the rows from front to back, personally handing the test grades back to each student. Anna and Lydia sat together at a table in the third row.

It took a while for Mr. Smith to reach their table. For Anna, it felt like half an eternity, and she became more anxious as the seconds ticked by. First, Mr. Smith gave Lydia her test grade.

He held Lydia's test in his hands, looked at the grade, and then said with a smile on his lips, "Very nicely done, Lydia! You performed the best! You didn't make a single mistake! Keep it up!"

Then, he happily laid the test on the table in front of Lydia. Once again, she earned an A. "Yay!" exclaimed Lydia with joy, and she beamed from ear to ear.
Mr. Smith was also obviously in a good mood, and he was happy for his favorite student.

Now, Mr. Smith began to look in the pile of paper for Anna's test grade. When he found it, his mood became more serious again. Mr. Smith placed the test on the table in front of Anna and bent down to her.

"I actually expected a better performance from you. What was going on?", Mr. Smith whispered in Anna's ear so that the other students couldn't hear him.
Anna now looked at the red F on her test and swallowed. "I ... I ... I don't know exactly what happened ..." Anna whispered back softly.

"Well, then, I guess you had a bad day. It can happen to anyone! I'm sure your will do better next time!" said Mr. Smith quietly. Then he stood upright again and went to the next student.

Anna looked at her test as if it was a venomous spider. Almost every sentence had a mistake marked by Mr. Smith.
She started to tear up. She didn't want to cry in front of her classmates. So, she

held back her tears and tried not to let any
emotions show.
She had never felt so sad in her entire life.

Fortunately, class was over soon.
Anna couldn't wait to finally be alone in
her room. On the way home, Anna thought
about what she should tell her parents.

Anna was ashamed she had made the worst grade. That's why she didn't want to mention the test. She quickly realized that wouldn't be a solution either. After all, Mom and Dad would find out eventually. Maybe at the parent-teacher conference on Friday, or, at the latest, when she received her report card for the school year.

Anna arrived home discouraged. Dad was still at work until 2:00 p.m., but Mom was already home and had made lunch for the family.

"Hello, Anna! I'm glad you're here. I cooked us spaghetti. We'll have applesauce for dessert. Let's eat right away while it's still warm! Dad's going to be a little late coming home from work today!" Mom said warmly and gave Anna a kiss on the forehead.

Although Anna had little appetite, she sat down at the table with her mother.
It didn't take long for Mom to notice Anna's sadness. She knew her daughter too well and knew something was wrong.
"What's the matter, sweetie? Why are you so quiet today?" she asked. Anna just shrugged her shoulders and remained silent.
"You know you can tell me anything that's on your mind, right? I'm your mother, after all! Did anything bad happen at school?" mom asked, stroking Anna's cheek lovingly.

Finally, Anna gathered her words and answered with tears in her eyes, "Yes, I got an F on my test! I don't know how that could have happened. I studied enough, but it was just too hard for me." Tears now began to stream down Anna's cheeks. Mom hugged her tightly to comfort her.

After Anna calmed down, Mom began to say, "Although you probably see it quite differently right now, I don't think a bad grade is the end of the world. And it's nothing to be ashamed of.
You did your best, and that's what really counts. I once got an F in school and was very sad. But failures are also part of life.

Everything can't always go perfectly, even if we want it to. You will certainly have the opportunity to improve your overall grade. It's not bad, my darling!"

"Yes, it's very bad!" Anna contradicted, completely upset. "After all, you have to do well in school so you can get a good job later on. Besides, I'm annoyed that Lydia always gets A's. She's always better than me! Why can't I be as smart as she is?"

Mom replied in a soft voice, "A grade says nothing about what you can accomplish in your life. If you have a dream, then the most important thing to do is to believe in yourself.

I will always love you no matter what grades you get. You are a wonderful girl. No grade in the world can change how much I love you because grades don't determine a person's worth!"

It took a little while for Anna to really understand what Mom had told her. Then, she wiped the tears from her face, took a deep breath, and said, "I love you too, Mom." Anna was glad to have such a great mom. She was relieved Mom didn't mind that she hadn't done well on the test.

In the afternoon, Dad finally came home from work. He told us he had often earned a bad grade and wasn't the best student. However, he has a job that makes him happy.

Mom and Dad were proud Anna was so brave and open with them about her fears.

From now on, Anna promised herself never to feel devastated by a bad grade again. After all, there are much more important things in life.

As Mom said so beautifully at noon: a grade does not determine the value of a person.

The New Challenge

"Brrrrr!" The alarm clock rang at exactly 6:30 a.m. – right on time – and Laura was lying in her bed, still quite sleepy. She would have liked to sleep a little longer.

She could hear the rain outside, pounding on the window panes. It was cloudy and rainy all weekend. This morning the clouds hung low, and a stormy wind blew through the treetops and bushes.

Actually, Laura didn't mind the rain. She went on a daily walk with her dog, Buddy, no matter what the weather was like. While her four-legged friend focused on sniffing the path, she enjoyed watching the raindrops dance in the puddles. Since it was Monday, and school was restarting after the break, she couldn't dilly-dally any longer.

Laura quickly dressed and ran to the kitchen. Mom was already setting the table and Laura was in charge of the cereal. She rushed to say, "Good morning!" and gave her mom a kiss on the cheek. Then, she immediately started chopping fruit, which she added into the oatmeal.

"Well, Laura, do you feel confident about your new commute to school?" asked Mom, smiling slightly. "After all, starting today, like many other students, you will be taking the train to school by yourself!" continued Mom.

Laura was nine years old and in the third grade. Her parents decided during the break that she was finally old enough to ride the train alone to the nearby town where her school was located.

Until now, Mom, and occasionally Dad,

usually drove her to school. But that was about to change. For Mom, it was often stressful in the mornings, since Laura's younger siblings, Anna and Philipp, needed help.

Her parents had prepared Laura for this new challenge. Of course, she had already taken the train several times. But never alone. Recently, Mom and Dad had shown her several times what she had to pay attention to when riding the train: where to buy the ticket, which track the right train was on, how to show the conductor the ticket, and where Laura should get off.

Actually, she was a little proud that she was now allowed to ride alone, but Laura was a reserved and shy girl. She had a lot of friends. Still, she sometimes found it difficult to approach strangers. When Laura meets another student, she is naturally open and quickly makes a friend. But approaching someone you don't know at all? That was not easy for Laura, and she felt insecure about it.

Laura wished so much that Mary and Samantha would also ride the train with her. They were her best friends. But Mary lived right next to the school, so she could walk. Samantha lived in a nearby village and always took the bus. So, Laura would ride the train, together with only strangers. That scared her.

"Oh, mom, can you please drive me to school one last time today? Please! It's raining!" Laura begged during breakfast and looked at her mom.

"No, my darling, we already discussed all that yesterday. I have already bought the ticket for you! I'm sure you can do it!" Mom replied with conviction.

Laura let out a big sigh and realized there was little point in continuing to discuss this topic with her mother. She realized at some point she would have to go to school on her own. Today was going to be that time. Besides, she was old enough now!

After breakfast, Laura said goodbye to her mom and younger siblings. She left, feeling queasy, but she managed to muster some confidence.

Laura walked to the train station, which was close to the apartment. Fortunately, it had stopped raining. Silently, she realized she really knew everything to look out for, after all. A little more courage arose within her, and her steps became quicker and more deliberate. To reach the station, she had to cross a busy street. A crosswalk and a traffic light eased her way. Before Laura crossed the street, she looked carefully to the left and right to check for cars. She had learned that from her parents.

"It's better to be safe than sorry!" her grandmother used to say. So, to be completely sure, she looked left and right one more time and confirmed the traffic light was really on green. Everything was fine! She walked briskly across the crosswalk, and she reached the train station.

The station suddenly seemed larger and more intense than usual. Many people bustled along the tracks. The sound of the arriving and departing trains drowned out the many conversations. Women, men, and children were abundant in number!

Impressed by the hustle and bustle, Laura looked for the track with the number four. From there, her train departed at 7:38 a.m. Right on time, it slowly rolled in and stopped with a loud hiss. Laura stood behind a group of passengers. An elderly gentleman opened the door by pressing a button.
Laura cautiously climbed the stairs and looked for a good seat.

The aisles were narrow and crowded. Some people simply stopped at the window and chatted animatedly. Others were reading the newspaper or looking at their cell phones. Most of the seats were already taken. Laura let her gaze wander over the many rows of seats. Where should she sit?

She definitely didn't want to spend the entire ride standing up. Slowly, she walked through the train car and realized she would have to ask someone if she could sit down.

Almost reaching the end of the train, Laura saw a girl sitting alone. She had her backpack on her lap and was staring out the window with a blank expression. Laura hesitated, but decided to ask the girl if she could sit there. Maybe she went to the same elementary school and was even happy to meet Laura? "It costs nothing to ask nicely!" Laura had once heard her grandma say.

"Good morning! Is the seat next to you still free?" asked Laura with a slight smile on her lips.
"Hello, yes, the seat is still free! You're welcome to sit next to me!" the girl replied,

visibly pleased. Laura took her backpack off her shoulders and sat down quickly because more people were pushing through the aisles behind her.

Then, she turned to the girl and said, "My name is Laura, by the way!"
"And I'm Antonia," the girl replied.
The two smiled briefly at each other and began talking about all sorts of things.
They hit it off right away and realized they had so many things in common. They went to the same school, only Antonia was already in the fourth grade. They also both enjoyed painting pictures and dancing.

The two girls talked to each other so eagerly that they almost forgot they had to get off the train. Together, they completed the last leg of the journey to school.

Laura was overjoyed and convinced she had made a new friend. They even agreed to sit next to each other on the train again tomorrow.

For Laura, this day was a wonderful experience. The first thing she realized was she could make her way to school completely on her own. So many concerns and fears had tormented her before.

She had managed to adapt to a new and difficult environment. More importantly, she overcame her fear of approaching someone and making new friends. She learned that in life you should be open to new challenges.

Laura overcame her shyness and that made her very proud. What a special and unique day!

I am brave and strong !

The Star

Twinkle, twinkle, little star,
How I wonder what you are,
Up above the world so high,
Like a diamond in the sky.

When the blazing sun is set,
And the grass with dew is wet,
Then you show your little light,
Twinkle, twinkle, all the night.

Then the traveler in the dark
Thanks you for your tiny spark,
He could not see where to go
If you did not twinkle so.

In the dark blue sky you keep,
And often through my curtains peep,
For you never shut your eye
Till the sun is in the sky.

As your bright and tiny spark
Lights the traveler in the dark,
Though I know not what you are,
Twinkle, twinkle, little star.

(by Jane Taylor)

Finally!

Hailey knew the whole song by heart.
Satisfied with herself and the world, she
closed her textbook and snuggled into her
beanbag chair.

Her eyes wandered around the room.
A little relaxation would do her some good.
Tomorrow, she was supposed to sing the
song "Twinkle, twinkle, little star" in front of
her entire music class.

Thinking about it made her stomach churn
with nervousness. All of her classmates
would stare at her, and her music teacher
would recognize even the smallest mistake.
So, if she suddenly forgot the lyrics –
that would be so embarrassing! Hailey's
mom helped her learn the song by heart.
Repeatedly, Hailey sang the song to her
mom, or she sang to herself in her bedroom.

Mostly, she didn't make any mistakes. Sometimes, she didn't hit a note correctly, or she forgot the words. Hailey always felt terrible when she messed up.

Mom comforted her every time and said encouragingly, "Oh, Hailey, don't put so much pressure on yourself. Everyone makes mistakes. Nothing and no one in the whole world is perfect."

Deep down, Hailey knew that her mother was right, of course. But still, she didn't want to make a mistake. She wanted to do everything perfectly, and tomorrow was her big day. After all, music was one of her favorite subjects, and she wanted to get an

A on her report card like last year.
So, she practiced every day for two weeks.
Of course, Mom was proud that Hailey was
so ambitious and could sing really well.
It didn't really matter to her whether Hailey
scored an A, B, or whatever grade on her
report card. The most important thing for
her was Hailey was happy and would not
lose her love of singing.

It was already evening, and Hailey laid down
in her bed in her pajamas. She wanted to
go to bed earlier than usual tonight so she
could be properly rested tomorrow. She had
her music book in her hands. Once again,
she read the lyrics carefully so she would not
forget a single line.

As she did every night, Mom came into
Hailey's bedroom to say good night before

she went to bed. She knew Hailey would be auditioning tomorrow, and she might have trouble sleeping because of her excitement. Therefore, Hailey's mom sat down briefly by her daughter's bed. She gently put her hand on Hailey's shoulder and then spoke in a soft voice, "Don't worry about tomorrow. You've prepared so well, and I'm sure everything will work out."

Hailey slowly raised her head. Of course, she had prepared herself well. That didn't change her anxiety. At first, Hailey thought about keeping her fear to herself, but she decided to talk openly with her mom about what was eating away at her. Hailey was convinced that it would feel good to finally talk to someone about her worries.
"A sorrow shared is a sorrow halved," mom always told her.

So, Hailey decided to confide in her mom about her feelings.

"I know I'm well-prepared, but still I'm afraid that I'll forget the lines, and the other kids will laugh at me!" Hailey said sadly.

Mom immediately replied, "Well, I can't imagine that anyone will laugh at you.

I'll let you in on a secret: The other kids are probably just as nervous as you are. That's perfectly normal and not a bad thing.

Even we adults sometimes experience situations where we feel very nervous.

However, you should go to sleep; otherwise, you won't be able to get out of bed tomorrow!"

Mom tenderly gave Hailey a kiss on the forehead. Then, she turned off the light and left the room.

Hailey felt a little better. She was relieved

and happy to speak with mom. Not long after that, Hailey fell asleep.

The next day, Hailey packed her school supplies for class, ate a hearty breakfast, and headed off to school. In the first hour, she had English lessons. Normally, she always followed the lessons with full attention and the greatest interest. Hailey liked school, but she had a hard time concentrating and staying on task that day. She was so excited and tense because she would soon sing in front of the whole class. She couldn't think about anything else. Luckily, she had music class during the next hour and the wait was finally over.

After the school bell rang for second period, Hailey's teacher, Mr. Richards, stood up and said to the children, "As discussed last week, today some of you will sing the song 'Twinkle, twinkle, little star.' I hope that all of you have mastered the lyrics and have practiced a bit at home. Which one of you wants to come forward first and perform the song?"

Immediately, the whole classroom went so quiet you could hear a pin drop. Most of the girls and boys tilted their heads down or directed their eyes out the window or to the wall. None of them wanted to start.

After about ten seconds of silence, which had felt more like ten minutes to Hailey, Mr. Richards continued, "All right. If none of you want to volunteer, then I'll just pick someone. You leave me no choice!"

After this sentence, you could literally feel the tension in the classroom. All the children were nervous. Hailey stared at her desk. Her heart began to pound faster and faster. There was no way she wanted to be the first to perform, so she said to herself in her mind, "Please not me. Please not me."

Finally, Mr. Richards spoke, "Hailey! Please come to the front and sing 'Twinkle, twinkle, little star' for us!"
"What a bummer! Why me?" thought Hailey, slightly annoyed. Then, with knees shaking and flushed cheeks, she walked forward

from her seat to the blackboard. The other children were visibly relieved that they were not first. Now, they all looked eagerly at Hailey. Hailey took a moment to calm herself down. She took a few deep breaths.
Then, she began to sing. During the first verse, she was still nervous, and you could hear a slight tremor in her voice.
Gradually, her fear became smaller and smaller. She sang the next two verses almost perfectly.

Then, it happened! A sudden halt!
How did it go on again? Hailey had forgotten how the last stanza began. Hundreds of times she practiced the text and never had a problem with the last verse. Today, of all days, at the crucial lesson in front of her teacher and all her classmates, she got stuck.

Hailey's heart raced, and she raised her eyes in despair.

Now, everyone was looking at her with wide eyes. No one laughed at her or made a stupid remark. Just as mom had told her.

Mr. Richards noticed Hailey was faltering and needed a little help to finish the last verse. "As your bright and tiny spark ..." said Mr. Richards, hoping to jog Hailey's memory again.

Immediately, Hailey could remember again. She now also sang the last verse from beginning to end without mistakes. "Very nicely sung, Hailey! Thank you very much! You may take your seat again!" said Mr. Richards delightedly.

Slowly, all the pressure fell off Hailey's shoulders, and she felt liberated.

Although she hadn't sung perfectly and had even forgotten the words, she felt pleased with herself. Now, it was the other children's turn, and she listened attentively.

After the lesson, she asked Mr. Richards what grade she earned. She got a B! Hailey smiled and was happy. How anxious she had been! She had finally made it, and no one had laughed. Hailey learned it wasn't so bad if you made a mistake every once in a while.

Hailey was very proud of herself for not letting her fear bring her down. Next time, it will certainly be easier for her to stand up in front of the whole class. And who knows?

Maybe one day she would sing before a crowd at a concert? Oh, dreams are a beautiful thing.

Hailey couldn't wait to tell her mom about everything. What an eventful day!

I am
confident!

Closing

Words

I hope you enjoyed the stories in this book.
Which one was your favorite story?
Which story did you find most exciting?
Which story did you learn the most from?

Maybe you read this book all by yourself.
That would be great! Even if your parents

read the stories to you, that's no problem.
I'm sure you'll learn to read more fluently
and quickly over the next few years.
Practice makes perfect!

Hopefully, this book has shown you that
you don't have to be afraid of challenges in
your life. You can accomplish anything if you
simply believe in yourself.

You are a wonderful girl.
Don't forget that!

Imprint

The author is represented by: Pisionary Publishing Ltd
Adrea Omirou Ave 17, Rose Gardens Block B Apt.218
Year of publication: 2022
Responsible for printing: Amazon

Inspiring Stories for Amazing Girls
Eva Kinsley
ISBN:
1st edition 2022

Made in United States
North Haven, CT
05 September 2022

23704751R00064